THE WORST SHOW-AND-TELL ever

BY RITA WALSH

ILLUSTRATED BY STAN TUSAN

little rainbow®
Troll Associates

Okay, I'll admit it. I can never remember to bring anything in for Show-and-Tell. I guess you could say I'm a Show-and-Tell washout.

One day I was so desperate, I spent five minutes talking about my lunch box. Jason was the only one who listened. He's always interested in anything that has to do with food.

That wasn't even as bad as the time I wowed the class by showing them some freckles on my arm that sort of look like a mouse, if I hold my elbow a certain way.

So of course I hadn't even thought of Show-and-Tell that day until Jeff gave us a preview of his motorcycle helmet at recess. He always had the neatest things for Show-and-Tell.

"Yo!" he called to me. "Want to try it on? It'll cost you a quarter."

That's when I tripped over The Rock.
It was gray with little silvery sparkles. I
sighed and put it in my pocket. It was going
to be another loser Show-and-Tell day after all.

While Jason was demonstrating how to eat a coconut, I tried to think of something cool to say about my rock. Then it came to me.

"It's a comet," I told the class.

"No, it isn't," said brainy Bridget McRooney, who always sounds just like a nerdy scientist. "It's an asteroid."

"No way!" said Brad. "I bet he found it in the parking lot."

"Maybe he just took it out of his head!" shouted Toni.

Whoops of laughter surrounded me as I shuffled back to my desk in disgrace. Jason almost choked on a piece of coconut. Even Mrs. Hogglefuss was chuckling a little bit.

This had to be the worst Show-and-Tell ever, I thought.

As I slunk deeper in my seat, Sal marched past me to the front of the room. He had made a volcano out of clay and filled it up with baking soda. Then he poured in some vinegar.

"Behold!" he whispered, as we all leaned forward to see what would happen.

Lava began to bubble up and run down the sides of the volcano.

"Salvatore!" said Mrs. Hogglefuss. "What a wonderful Show-and-Tell!"

While we were all looking at the volcano, there was a loud pop from the back of the room. My asteroid had exploded!

"We're here!" cried a squeaky little voice. Two little space creatures climbed out of the rock and pointed at the volcano.

"Martians!" screamed the twins, Sharen and Karen.

"There is no such thing as a Martian," said Bridget, rolling her eyes.

"Outta sight!" shouted Jeff, taking off his sunglasses. "Cool Show-and-Tell!"

For once in my life, I had impressed him.

But I didn't have any time to enjoy being the new Show-and-Tell king because those two little Martians ran right out of the classroom.

Mrs. Hogglefuss flung herself across her desk to get out of their way. "Mayday!" she shouted. "Mayday!"

The whole class chased the Martians into the gym, where the track team was running laps. The runners all screamed and jumped into the bleachers. Only Coach Burley didn't move— he was too busy timing the Martians in the 50-meter sprint!

"The Martians broke the record! The
Martians broke the record!" he screamed,
jumping up and down.

But those Martians didn't slow down a bit.
They ran straight for the cafeteria.

Greasy Joe was cooking up some kind of spaghetti. All those big pots of bubbling gunk must have looked just like home to the aliens. One Martian dived headfirst into one of the pots. The other Martian did a cannonball.

Just then the police burst through the doors.
"Put your hands up!" they ordered.

Greasy Joe threw his hands up in the air,
splattering spaghetti sauce all over Mrs.
Hogglefuss.

Coach Burley finally caught up with us. "Don't you dare arrest those Martians!" he huffed. "They just broke the record for the 50-meter sprint!"

Everyone started cheering. Our school had never broken any records—EVER! Jason even stopped slurping spaghetti long enough to burp with joy.

Principal Van Munzhoffer promptly enrolled the Martians as foreign exchange students. Sal let them live in his volcano. Bridget wrote an article for a science magazine about life on other planets. And Greasy Joe made them spaghetti every day.

Well, you can probably guess the rest. With the Martians on our track team, our school won every track meet that season. Coach Burley was named Coach of the Year. He even got his picture on the front page of the newspaper, right next to an article about a dog that could add and subtract.

So of course no one was surprised when our school was renamed "Martian Academy." It was a very moving ceremony, and when Principal Van Munzhoffer introduced the Martians, all the teachers and parents were bawling their eyes out.

I guess I got a little choked up, too.

But do you know what bothered me about the whole thing? No one remembered that the Martians had been part of my Show-and-Tell project! No one!

Even the Martians seemed to forget that they owed all their fame and glory to me. They started wearing sunglasses and hanging out with Jeff all the time. Soon I became just another one of their adoring fans.

But at least I never forget Show-and-Tell day anymore.